Here comes John

For Angus

Copyright©1983 by Bob Graham

Library of Congress Catalog Card No. 88–80589

ISBN 0–316–32305–5
10   9   8   7   6   5   4   3   2   1

First published in Great Britain in 1984
by Hamish Hamilton Children's Books

Printed in Hong Kong by
South China Printing Co.

Here comes John

Bob Graham

Little, Brown and Company
Boston   Toronto

Here comes a snail.

It's in a hurry.
Look at it go!

Look out, snail!

It's dangerous
crossing the path.

The ground is shaking.
Something is coming!

Look at the snail go.
Look at its silver trail.

Here comes Theo.

Theo has missed it.

Here comes Sarah.

Sarah has missed it.

Here comes John.

John sees it,

because John spends
a lot of time

on his hands and knees.

The snail spends
a lot of time

curled up in
its protective shell.

John likes to feel
and taste everything.

He picks up the snail . . .

now it's heading straight
for John's mouth.

LOOK OUT, SNAIL!

Sarah sees him.

"NO, JOHN," shouts Sarah.

"Snails are for gardens,
not for mouths.

"Put it back, John."

John rises slowly to his feet,

he sways, and
drops the snail.

Down goes the snail,

curled up tightly
in its shell.

When it feels safe again,
it will crawl into
the damp, dark leaves.